DOGS AND DANGER

JUDITH BAUER STAMPER

 SPRINT BOOKS

 SCHOLASTIC BOOK SERVICES
New York Toronto London Auckland Sydney Tokyo

Photographs by Richard Hutchings

This book is from Spring Library 3B.
Other titles in this library are:
The Mystery of the Jade Princess
Star Jewel
Strange Friends
Pier 92

ISBN 0-590-30537-9
Copyright © 1979 by Judith Bauer Stamper. All rights reserved. Published by Scholastic Book Services, a division of Scholastic Magazines, Inc.
12 11 10 9 8 7 6 5 4 3 2 1 9 9/7 0 1 2 3 4/8
12
Printed in the U.S.A.

DOGS AND DANGER

CHAPTER

"Where are you going?" Kate's mother asked.

Kate answered her mother as she ran out the door. "Over to see Dr. Marx. I'll be back for dinner."

The door banged shut behind her. Kate didn't hear her mother say anything more. She smiled and ran to her bike.

Dr. Marx lived ten blocks from Kate's house. He was a veterinarian with a small animal hospital next to his house. Kate often rode over to help him after school. She loved animals.

Kate turned her bike onto Dr. Marx's street. She pedalled hard, then coasted for a while. Kate liked riding fast, with the fall breeze blowing in her face.

In a few minutes, she came to Dr. Marx's house. She saw a car parked there. Dr. Marx was probably taking care of an animal.

Kate leaned her bike against the side of the building. She slipped into the office through the back door. Dr. Marx was standing over his work table. He had a long needle in his hand. A black cat was on the table. Its green eyes were staring at the needle. Kate could see that

this cat didn't want a shot.

Dr. Marx glanced up and saw Kate. "It's a good thing you're here, Kate. I've got a scared cat on the table and a scared owner in the waiting room. Can you calm the cat while I prepare his medicine?"

Kate went over to the table. Gently, she began to stroke the cat's black fur. Dr. Marx went to prepare the shot.

"Kitty, why are you scared?" Kate asked softly. She rubbed her thumb under the cat's ear and he began purring.

Dr. Marx heard it and chuckled. "Kate, I think you could make a tiger purr."

Kate kept talking to the cat. Dr. Marx came back to the table. Then Kate stroked the cat some more, and he closed his green eyes. Dr. Marx gently pushed the needle and the shot was over.

"You can tell the owner her cat survived the operation," Dr. Marx said with a grin.

Kate ran and told the owner. She was very happy as she picked up her cat. Then she paid her bill and left.

"Well, Kate," said Dr. Marx. "It looks like a quiet afternoon." But just then a car pulled up into the driveway. It screeched to a fast stop. "I spoke too soon," said the doctor.

There was a knock on the door. A young man

came in, carrying a cocker spaniel. The dog's right front paw was wrapped in a rag. Blood was seeping through it.

"Doc, the dog's paw is cut bad," said the man. "He caught it in a lawn mower."

Kate watched as Dr. Marx put the dog on the table. Then the telephone rang. He had to go answer it.

"Hold the dog, Kate, will you?" he said.

Kate tried to calm the poor dog. He was in bad pain.

"You think it has been poisoned?" Kate heard Dr. Marx ask.

Kate looked up.

"I see. Can you bring the dog over immediately?" Dr. Marx looked worried. "I can't leave the office now. Are you sure you can't come over for the medicine?" Suddenly Dr. Marx turned to Kate. "Kate, do you have your bicycle here?"

Kate nodded her head.

"Could you ride to Market Street in ten minutes?"

"Sure," Kate answered. "I could cut through the park."

"That would probably be faster than a car," Dr. Marx said. Then he spoke into the phone. "My helper will be coming with the medicine in ten minutes. The instructions will be written on the bottle."

Dr. Marx hung up and went to the medicine cabinet. Kate patted the dog as Dr. Marx worked.

"All right, Kate. Here it is. Take this bottle to Mr. Hillman on Market Street. He owns the gift shop. Do you know where it is?"

"Sure. I've been there a lot," Kate said. She carefully took the medicine and put it in her shirt pocket. She buttoned the flap to be safe.

"Thanks, Kate," Dr. Marx said. "I have to stay and help this spaniel. I'll come over to Mr. Hillman's store as soon as I can."

Kate raced out the door to her bike. She knew just the path to take. It cut through the park so there wouldn't be any cars.

She pedalled her bike as hard as she could. After some hard riding she saw the park straight ahead.

"The medicine!" she thought suddenly. Was it still in her pocket? She patted to feel the small bottle. It was still there.

Kate rode her bike on the path. It was taking too long to get there.

"It's up to me," Kate whispered to herself. "I've got to make it on time. The dog needs the medicine *now*."

Kate's bike shot through the fallen leaves on the path. She didn't slow down or coast. She

pedalled harder, and soon she reached the end of the park. Market Street was near. It was only two blocks away.

The streets were busy with traffic, but Kate quickly got across them. She pulled up in front of Mr. Hillman's store.

"I hope I didn't take too long," she thought. She ran into the store and almost bumped into Mr. Hillman.

Kate saw the worried look on his face. He looked very sad too. "Is...is your dog still alive?" she asked.

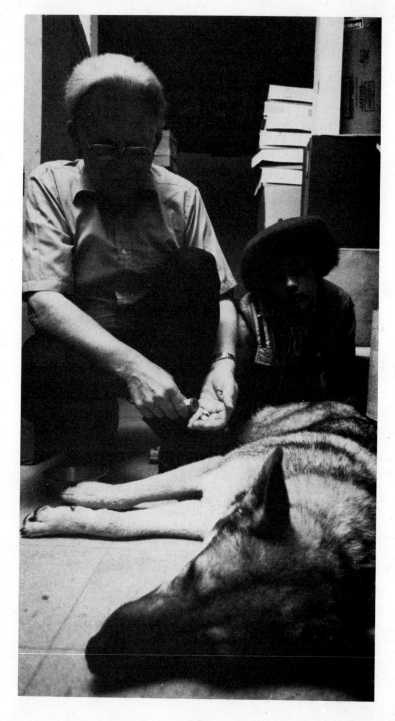

CHAPTER 2

"She's still alive," Mr. Hillman said. "But she's awfully sick."

Kate followed him into the back room. She pulled out the medicine from her shirt and handed it to Mr. Hillman.

"You got here pretty fast. Thank you," Mr. Hillman said. He began reading the instructions on the bottle. Kate looked at the German shepherd lying on the floor. Its eyes were watery and its tongue was an ugly color. She wanted to pet the dog and comfort it. But she decided she'd better not.

Mr. Hillman shook two pills from the bottle. Then he turned to Kate.

"I need your help," he said. "But I don't even know your name."

"My name is Kate. What can I do?"

"Kate, I want you to pet the dog's sides while I give her the medicine. Her name is Penny."

"Poor Penny," Kate whispered as she stroked the dog's brown fur.

Mr. Hillman worked the pills into the dog's mouth. Then he put a dish of water up to it. "I think the pills went down," he said with relief.

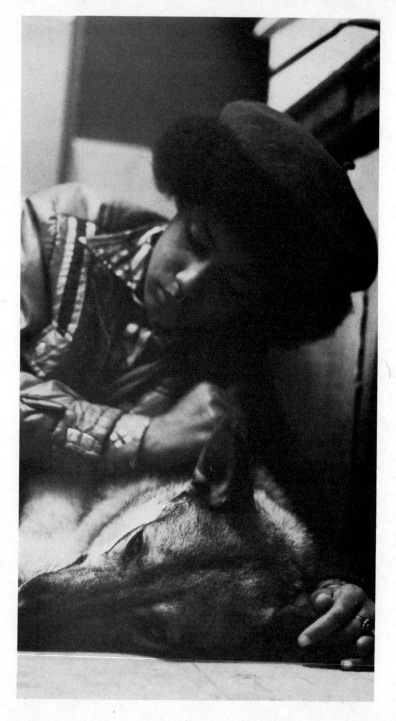

"That's all Dr. Marx told me to do. We'll just have to wait it out."

Kate looked at her watch. It was 4:30. She should be getting home for dinner. But when she looked at Penny again, she couldn't leave. She had to find out if Penny would survive.

For the next half hour, Kate sat with her. Mr. Hillman went back into the store to wait on customers. Kate was glad she could comfort Penny. The dog was too sick to be left alone.

Finally, Dr. Marx came in. Kate was sitting there, stroking Penny's side.

"I see the dog has a good nurse," said Dr. Marx. "Now, let's see how she's doing." He bent down and examined Penny's eyes and mouth and stomach. Kate watched nervously.

"Did the pills go down all right?" the doctor asked Kate.

"I think so. Mr. Hillman didn't have any trouble with them."

"Well, then I think the dog should be fine. She got most of the poison out of her stomach right away. And the medicine should take care of whatever is left."

Kate felt relieved. Just then, Mr. Hillman rushed into the room.

"Is she all right, doctor?" The doctor told him Penny would pull through. They had done everything that they could. Now her body would have to heal itself.

"Do you know how she got hold of the poison?" Dr. Marx asked.

Mr. Hillman sighed and shook his head. "I wish I did. Penny is my guard dog. She's more important to me than just a pet. This afternoon I found her in the back alley. She was sicker than she's ever been. Then I saw some meat nearby. The poison was wrapped inside it."

Dr. Marx shook his head. "Who would do something like that?"

"Maybe somebody wants to get rid of Penny," Kate said. She was curious and angry.

"Penny isn't a mean dog," Mr. Hillman said. He bent down to pet her.

"I'm afraid I have to go now, Mr. Hillman," Dr. Marx said. "I'll check on Penny again tomorrow."

Kate glanced at her watch. "It's 5:30! I should be getting home."

"Thanks again, Kate," Mr. Hillman said as Kate rushed from the room.

"I'll be back, Mr. Hillman," Kate called to him. "Good-bye, Dr. Marx."

She jumped on her bike and pedalled home as fast as she could. It looked like she had to race everywhere today.

Kate pulled the bike into her backyard. She looked at her watch. It was almost six o'clock

now. Her mother and father always ate dinner at six. Kate walked into the kitchen, knowing trouble was ahead.

"Hello, Kate," said her mother. "I'm glad you could make it home for dinner."

Kate smiled nervously and slipped into her chair. Was her mother angry or kidding her? Kate's father passed her a big plate of fried chicken. "All right, Kate," he said. "Why are you so late?"

"Well, I was at Dr. Marx's and he had to care for a cocker spaniel and then the telephone...." The words rushed out of Kate's mouth.

"Slow down, Kate. You can tell us while you eat your dinner," her father said.

Kate felt better. She helped herself to some chicken. Then, over the meal, she told her parents about Penny.

"Who would do such a mean thing?" Kate's mother asked.

"I'd like to find out," Kate said.

"I think you have had enough excitement, Kate," said her father. "You know, sometimes I worry about you. Other girls have friends and do things together. I know you help Dr. Marx. But maybe you should be with kids your own age."

Kate looked down at her food. She had heard all this before from her father. "I don't go over just to see Dr. Marx. I like helping the animals," Kate said.

Kate's mother gave her father a long look. "Maybe if Kate had her own pet...," she began to say.

Kate looked at her father hopefully. But he said the same thing as always. "I don't think Kate has gotten over Bonnie yet."

A lump rose in Kate's throat. It was true. She wasn't over Bonnie yet. Bonnie had been her

pet collie for five years. Kate got her on her sixth birthday. Then, three months ago, Bonnie had been killed.

Kate pushed her chair away from the table. "May I leave for a minute, Mom? I'll be back to do the dishes."

"Yes, Kate," said her mother.

Kate walked outside and let the wind blow on her face. She still felt terrible about Bonnie. And it had been her fault!

CHAPTER 3

Kate stopped by to see Mr. Hillman after school the next day. When Kate saw Penny she smiled. "You're doing a lot better," she said. Kate bent down and petted the German shepherd's smooth coat.

"Kate, is that you?" Mr. Hillman called from the back room.

"Yes, Mr. Hillman. I came to see how Penny's doing."

Mr. Hillman walked into the front of the store. His hands were loaded with small boxes. "I was just in the back room, getting new stock for the shelves. As you can see, Penny is doing her job again. She's acting as good as new."

Kate could see that it was true. Penny's eyes were bright and her tongue looked pink and healthy. "She had a close call, though, didn't she?" Kate said to Mr. Hillman.

"Well, thanks to you and Dr. Marx," Mr. Hillman said, "she pulled through. I couldn't run the shop without her."

"What do you mean?" Kate asked.

"I need Penny to watch things when I go into the back room. Or if I leave the store. She has a real nose for trouble. If she trusts a customer,

21

she just lies quietly. But if she suspects someone, she sure lets me know."

"I guess she trusts me," Kate said. "She didn't bark when I came in the door."

"She trusts you all right," Mr. Hillman said. "But I wish she hadn't been sick yesterday. She could have warned me about the people who were here."

"What do you mean?" Kate saw that Mr. Hillman was getting upset.

"There were shoplifters in the store yesterday," Mr. Hillman said. "They stole some goods. It happened while I was in the back room with Penny."

"What did they steal?" Kate asked. She really felt sorry for Mr. Hillman. Yesterday was such a bad day for him.

"They went for the expensive things. They always do. They took an electric shaver and a bottle of good perfume."

"Oh, no," Kate said. Just then Penny let out a whimper. "What's wrong, Penny?" Kate asked. "Do you feel sick?"

Mr. Hillman smiled. "No, she just knows I'm upset. Well, there was nothing you could do about it, Penny. It wasn't your fault."

Just then a customer came in and started looking around.

"I'd better help this customer, Kate. But you

can stay awhile if you would like to."

"Thanks, Mr. Hillman," Kate said. "But I'd better be going."

"Are you going to Dr. Marx's to help him out?"

"No," Kate answered. Her voice sounded disappointed. "My dad said I should stay in the park this afternoon. He wants me to meet kids my own age."

"Well, go ahead and enjoy yourself." Mr. Hillman went over to help the woman. Kate reached down and petted Penny good-bye.

She walked out of the store and down Market Street toward the park. Last year after school she was always with Alice. They had grown up together on the same block, and they had always been best friends. But last spring, Alice's family moved to another city. And Kate didn't have a new friend yet. She had started helping Dr. Marx over the summer — right after Bonnie was killed.

Kate ran into the park. A group of boys and girls passed her on skateboards. They were laughing and having fun. Kate felt even more alone watching them.

"Boy, I really miss you, Alice," she whispered to herself. Kate kept walking on the path. Then she saw some girls from her school. They were doing cartwheels. Kate watched them for a while.

"Hi, Kate! Want to do cartwheels with us?" a girl named Julie called out.

Kate blushed. I don't know how to turn a cartwheel, she said to herself. "Thanks, but I need to get home," Kate called back. She smiled at Julie and hurried away.

Kate thought she might as well go home. She could always help her mother fix dinner.

Then Kate saw something that made her stop
walking. Some kids were ahead of her, playing
with a collie. There were three of them — two

boys and a girl. They all looked older than Kate. There was a collar around the dog's neck with a lead chain attached to it.

Kate watched as one of the boys jerked at the chain. The collie cried with pain. Kate just couldn't stand there and watch. She ran up to the boy holding the lead.

"You're hurting the dog!" Kate said. "Can't you see that?"

The boy stared at her, surprised. "What business is it..." he started to say. But the girl they were with stopped him.

"Do you know anything about dogs?" she asked Kate.

"I had a collie for five years," Kate answered.

"Maybe you could teach us to use this collar and lead," the girl said. She gave the boy a mean look.

"We sure could use some help," the other boy said.

Kate didn't like the way these kids looked. She had never seen them before. But she felt sorry for the collie.

"Sure, I can help...the dog." The boy handed Kate the lead. She reached down and touched the collie.

"What is its name?"

"Major," the girl answered.

"OK, Major. Let's go for a walk," Kate said. She pulled gently on the lead. The collie got up.

Kate walked him around for ten minutes, and showed the girl how to use the lead.

"Take good care of your dog," Kate told them before she left. "He's beautiful."

"Thanks," the girl said. "We'll see you around here again sometime."

"Maybe," Kate said as she walked away. She'd never forgive the boy for being so cruel.

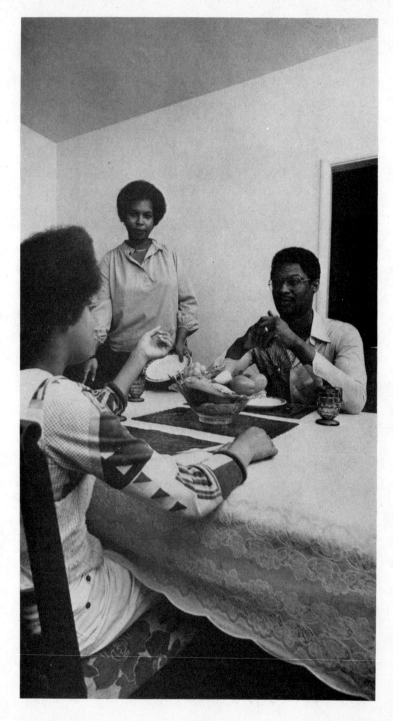

CHAPTER 4

"What did you do after school today, Kate?"

Kate glanced across the table at her father. She knew he'd ask her that question. She was ready with her answer. "First, I stopped in at Mr. Hillman's store. I wanted to check on Penny."

"Is she all right?" asked Kate's mother.

"Penny is back in the store, and she looks pretty good. Mr. Hillman uses her as a guard dog, you know."

"Then where did you go?" asked her father. He was determined to hear what he wanted to hear.

"Then," Kate continued, "I went to the park. And I talked with some kids who had a beautiful collie. I taught them how to use a lead on the dog." Kate stopped and smiled at her parents. Her father couldn't complain about that.

"Are all the questions finished now?" Kate's mother said to her father. Then she turned and faced Kate. "You know, we just want you to be happy, Kate. We think you should make some new friends."

Kate shrugged. "I liked the collie better than the kids. It was so much fun walking him. And you know what? He even looked a little like Bonnie." She paused and said, "Poor Bonnie."

"You're going to have to forget about Bonnie, Kate," her father said. "What happened to her was an accident. Even the driver of the car said so. He admitted he was driving too fast."

"But I was the one who called her," Kate answered. "She dashed across the street because of me. It was all my fault." Kate had lived Bonnie's death a million times over in her mind. If only she had looked down the street first. But she hadn't. She had whistled and Bonnie had come running. Then the car hit the collie. And it was all over.

"I know you'd like another dog, Kate," said her father. "But we think you're not quite ready yet. When you forget what happened to Bonnie...and when you find some new friends...then we'll talk about it."

No one said anything for a while. Kate finished eating the food on her plate.

"Mom, could I go over to Dr. Marx's now?" she asked. "Just for a little while? I know he has office hours tonight. And I finished all my homework in school."

"Go ahead," said her mother. "Your father can help with the dishes."

"Thanks, Mom," she said as she got up from the table.

There weren't any cars in Dr. Marx's driveway when Kate rode up on her bike. "Dr. Marx, are you here?" Kate called from the back door.

"Come in, Kate, come in," he answered.

Kate walked into the room. There wasn't much light. Kate needed a while to get used to the dark.

"You've come just in time, Kate," said Dr. Marx. "Rosebud is having her first litter. It's something to see."

Kate walked over to the corner of the room. There, snuggled in the box, was a tiger cat. Beside her was a tiny kitten, newly born.

"It's so small," Kate said.

"Yes, it is," Dr. Marx smiled. "Move back a little now, Kate. You don't want to upset a new mother. She needs room."

Kate stepped back a little and sat down on the floor.

"Why is Rosebud having kittens here, Dr. Marx? Is there some problem?"

"Nothing is wrong," he answered. "Her owners had to leave town this morning. But they knew that something was going to happen soon. So they brought her here."

"Oh!" Kate gasped. And while she watched,

another tiny kitten was born.

"Do you think that's all?" Kate asked.

Dr. Marx gently touched the cat's stomach. "No, I think we'll see another kitten soon." Then he got up. "I have some work to do in the next room, Kate. You can stay here and watch."

Kate had to strain her eyes to see clearly. The room was getting darker and darker as the sun was setting. Everything was very quiet.

Kate sat beside the box, not moving. Soon she saw another small head emerge from the mother cat.

"This one is gold," Kate called out to Dr. Marx.

"So was its father, I imagine," answered the doctor.

Now all three kittens were getting milk from their mother. Kate finally got up to leave. She had totally lost all track of time.

"That was something!" she said, "But I guess I'd better be getting home now. Dad will wonder what happened to me."

"Have you talked to him about getting another dog, Kate?" asked Dr. Marx.

"Yes, I have," Kate answered. "I just mentioned it again tonight. But he just said no again."

"I think I know why your father said no. It's because you still feel guilty about Bonnie. But it wasn't your fault she was struck by that car."

"No, I guess not," Kate whispered. Her voice sounded like she didn't mean it, though.

Dr. Marx gave Kate a stern look. "You have to learn to trust yourself, Kate. When you do, you'll be ready for another dog."

"OK, Dr. Marx," Kate said. "I'd better be getting home now." Kate left the office and rode home slowly. Maybe the doctor is right,

she thought. Maybe it wasn't my fault that Bonnie died. Then she thought of Penny. She had certainly helped Penny! She knew she had. That made Kate feel a lot better.

"Something will happen," Kate whispered to herself. "Something will happen to prove I'm ready."

CHAPTER 5

After school the next day, Kate started walking home. She was going through the playground, when a girl called her.

"Hey, Kate, wait up a minute."

Kate turned around. It was Julie calling her. They had worked together in math class that afternoon.

Julie ran up and walked beside Kate. "I'm going to the park," she said. "Want to come along?"

Kate had planned on going straight home. But she changed her mind fast. "Sure, I'd like to," she answered.

Julie smiled. "I'm meeting Susan and Ellen there. We're going to practice gymnastics."

Kate's heart sank. She wanted to get to know Julie better. But she couldn't do it with the others around. Suddenly she felt left out again.

"You'll come with us, won't you, Kate?" Julie asked. They were getting nearer to the park.

"I don't think so. I'm not very good at that sort of thing." Kate was still afraid to do gymnastics in front of everybody. The girls might laugh at her.

"Well, come and watch us, at least," Julie said. "What sort of things do you like to do?"

"I love being with animals," said Kate.

Julie's eyes lit up. "I've got a new dog, a Scottie," she said. "I'll bring it to the park sometime."

"That would be great!" said Kate.

Just then, Julie's other friends came by. "Susan, Ellen, over here," Julie called. Soon the three of them were doing back bends and head stands. Kate sat on the grass and watched. It was boring for her, though. She wished she were at Dr. Marx's instead.

Kate sat watching with her back to the sidewalk. Some kids were coming up the walk and talking. Their voices sounded familiar.

"I think it was a horrible thing to do," a girl said.

"It got what it deserved," a boy's voice snarled.

"But poison is going too far!" The girl sounded angry.

Kate's eyes opened wide! The girl had said POISON! She strained her ears to hear more. But they were walking away from her now. All she could hear were footsteps and the padding of a dog's paws on the sidewalk.

Kate turned around slowly and took a quick look. She saw the three kids she had talked

with yesterday. And they had the collie with them again.

One of the boys saw Kate. "Hey, it's you," said the boy. "What's your name?"

"Kate," she answered. The collie ran up to Kate and rubbed its nose on her hand.

"Hi, Major, what do you want?" Kate asked. The collie kept rubbing her hand. Kate laughed and finally started petting him.

"He never does that for me," complained one of the boys. He was the same one who tugged Major's chain the other day. The same one that the girl had been arguing with just now.

Kate looked up at him. "Maybe the dog doesn't trust you."

The boy laughed. "I could care less." His face looked mean.

The girl leaned down to pet the collie, too. "My name is Tracy. This is Mike and Pete," she said, pointing to the boys. "Would you like to walk Major with us awhile?"

Kate glanced back at Julie and the other girls. They didn't pay any attention to her. And, besides, Kate was curious about these kids. What sort of poison were they talking about? Did it have anything to do with Penny?

Kate got up from the ground. "Sure, I'd love to walk Major," she said.

Tracy handed the lead to her, and they all

walked down the path together.

"What's that thing around Major's neck?" Kate asked. She had noticed a leather pouch hanging from his collar.

The boys looked at each other and laughed. Tracy turned around and gave them both a funny look. They quieted down.

"Oh, we just put things in it," Tracy said. Kate felt she wasn't telling the truth.

"Valuable things," Mike said. Then he snickered. Kate looked at Mike. He was the mean one.

"We're trying to train Major," Pete said. "Maybe you could help us."

"How about it, Kate?" asked Tracy.

"I guess I can," Kate answered. Should she stay with them? She hated being around these kids. But maybe she would find out something. Kate kept thinking of Penny lying on the floor, sick—from poison. That made her angry.

"This is what we want Major to do," Pete began to explain. He turned to Tracy. "Walk over to that tree." He pointed to a tree a few yards away. "I'll unfasten Major's lead from his collar," Pete said. He bent down and did it. "Now, I want Major to run over to Tracy." Pete stamped his foot in front of Major. "Run!" he commanded. Major looked at him. He just sat there on the sidewalk.

"Why won't the dumb dog run?" Mike asked. He sounded angry.

Kate knelt down beside Major. She petted him and gently said his name over and over. Then she walked a few feet away. "Here, Major," she called. She gave a short whistle, and the dog ran up to her.

"Hey, pretty good," Tracy said. "Try it again, farther away."

Kate did the exercise over and over. Each time, she went farther away from Major. Soon she didn't even use his name. She gave the short whistle and Major came running. Each time he did it, Kate rewarded him with a friendly pat.

"Now, let me try it," Pete said. "Let's see if Major comes to me." Pete walked a long way off, and gave a loud whistle. But Major wouldn't move. He sat right where he was.

Mike and Tracy looked over at Kate. "I guess Major only comes to me," she said.

"Listen, Kate," Mike said, smiling. "Would you like to join us in a game we play?"

"What kind of game?" Kate asked. I don't like his smile, she said to herself. I don't trust him at all.

"I'll tell you about it tomorrow," he said. "Meet us on the corner of Market and Vine Streets at four o'clock. Then we can show you our game."

Kate was scared. These kids might be dangerous. But this was her chance to learn about Penny. Had they poisoned her? If they had, she wouldn't let them get away with it.

"OK," Kate said. "I'll meet you there tomorrow." Her heart pounded hard as she ran all the way home.

CHAPTER 6

Kate looked down at her watch. It was two minutes to four. She was standing on Market Street, near the corner of Vine. Tracy, Pete, and Mike were nowhere in sight.

Maybe they wouldn't be coming after all. If they did, Kate didn't want anyone to see her with them. These kids weren't very nice. Kate's parents wouldn't want them to be her friends.

"Kate, come over here." It was Mike's voice behind her. Kate quickly turned around. Tracy was standing across the street, with Major on a lead. Mike and Pete were standing on the corner.

"Kate, get over here," Mike called again, impatiently.

Kate crossed the street with Mike and Pete. They met Tracy on the opposite side.

"Kate, I'm glad you could come," said Tracy. Kate smiled weakly at her. I wish I knew what's going to happen, she said to herself.

"Let's take a little walk," said Mike. "Then I can tell you all about our game. You'll have a big part in it, Kate." They turned down Vine Street and went toward the park.

"Maybe you'd better walk Major," Tracy said. She handed Kate the lead. Kate took it and patted the dog's head. She noticed that the leather pouch was hanging around Major's neck again. She had to find out what was in it. Maybe it was poison!

"Where are we going?" Kate asked.

"I just felt like getting off Market Street," Mike said.

Kate started thinking fast. Why won't they walk on Market Street? Is it because of Mr. Hillman and Penny? Kate got brave all of a sudden. She took a deep breath and said, "Do you know Mr. Hillman?"

Suddenly Mike stopped walking. "Sure, I know old man Hillman. A lot of people do. Why do you ask?"

Kate stayed calm. "Oh, I just wondered," she said. "I know him, too." Kate noticed that Tracy was looking at her closely. She'd better not say anything else. Mike didn't like it when she said Mr. Hillman's name. He had really acted strange.

Mike turned into an alley. "Listen," he said. "It's getting late. Kate, this is what I want you to do." The four of them formed a circle. Mike leaned against a concrete wall along the alley. Then he pulled some chalk from his pocket and drew a map on the wall. It showed the streets between Market Street and the park.

"Kate, this is a little game we play," he said.

"It's like a relay race," Pete added. "You know, when runners hand something to each other in a race?"

"That's right," said Mike. "A relay race." He had a smile on his face. "We decided to include Major in our race. And that's where you come in, Kate."

I don't think I like this, Kate told herself.

Mike pointed the chalk at Kate. "Major listens to your commands. So he'll run his part of the race to you. You'll be waiting for him near the park.

Mike put an "X" where Kate was supposed to stand. It was on Elm Street, a block from the park.

"Where will everybody else be?" asked Kate.

Mike drew another "X" on the map. "Tracy will stay here with Major. It is five blocks from

you. Major can still hear you whistle from
there."

Kate studied the map. "But how will I know
when to whistle?"

"When you see me," Mike said. "I'll come up
to Tracy and the dog. Wait two minutes after
that. Then whistle."

"OK," Kate said. This sounded like a stupid
game. Or was it a game? Maybe it was
something worse. "Where will Pete be?" she
asked.

"Pete will stay with you," Mike said. "At least this time. Now everybody go to your places."

Kate and Pete went to Elm Street. "What did Mike mean when he said 'this time'?" she asked him.

"I don't know," Pete said. "Maybe he means until we can trust you."

Kate looked at Pete sideways. What did that mean? she thought. "Trust me with what?" she asked.

Pete kicked a stone down the street. "Trust you to call Major," he answered.

Kate could see that Pete was lying. Maybe Mike and Pete suspected her already. She shouldn't have asked about Mr. Hillman. Kate felt better being with Pete than with Mike. Soon they arrived at the place where they were supposed to wait. They could see Tracy and Major five blocks up the street.

Thoughts kept racing through Kate's mind. I'm going to ask Pete about the poisoning, she decided. He might tell me since we're alone. "Pete, why did Mike get upset when I mentioned Mr. Hillman's name?"

Pete still seemed calm. "Mike had a problem with Mr. Hillman's dog," Pete answered. "Do you know that big German shepherd he keeps in the store?"

Kate nodded her head. She wanted Pete to keep talking. She had to know the truth — even if it was terrible.

"Well, the dog tried to bite Mike once," Pete said. "But Mike got back at it — almost."

Kate's heart pounded faster and faster. "What do you mean?" she asked.

"He...," Pete stopped. "Mike is coming up the street," he said.

Kate looked up Elm Street. Mike was bending down near Major. He had his hands around Major's neck. But Kate couldn't see what he was doing. Then he stood up and walked away. Tracy waved.

"That's your signal, Kate," said Pete. "Give Major his whistle."

Kate wet her lips, and let out a loud, clear whistle. Major came running to her. His tail wagged as he ran up to Kate.

"Good dog, Major," she said. She got down and hugged him.

"It worked," Pete said. He looked happy. "Now both of us have to take Major this way." Pete started down the street to the park. "Come on, Kate, hurry up," he called. "The game isn't over."

Kate was still petting Major. "Wait a minute, Pete," she called. "What's in here?" She pointed to Major's leather pouch. The bag

looked fuller than before. Did they just put something in it?

"That's none of your business, Kate," Pete said. "Come on. I said the game isn't over."

Kate stood up. "I have to get home now," she said. Then she walked down the street fast.

What was in that pouch? Kate remembered what Mr. Hillman had said about shoplifters. Did these kids have something to do with that? She had to find out.

CHAPTER 7

Kate didn't tell anyone about the relay race. She had to talk to Mr. Hillman first. There was something she had to find out. She went straight to his store after school the next day.

"Kate, I'm glad you stopped in to visit again," Mr. Hillman said. Penny got up and walked over to Kate.

"Penny's gained a little weight," Kate said. "She must be over the poison now."

Mr. Hillman came out from behind the counter. "Yes, Penny won't have trouble with that again. She knows what made her sick."

"Is everything all right with the store?" Kate asked Mr. Hillman. That was really what she wanted to know.

"Of course. Things are all right, Kate. What do you mean?" he asked.

"I just wondered," Kate answered. Then she said what was most on her mind. "Have shoplifters bothered you lately, Mr. Hillman?"

"Why no, Kate." He looked surprised. "But I heard Penny growl yesterday afternoon. I was in the back room at the time. When I came out, the store was empty."

59

Kate sighed with relief. Maybe those kids weren't shoplifters after all. Maybe she was wrong.

Suddenly the shop door opened, and a man came in.

"Hello, Mr. Kastan. What can I do for you?" Mr. Hillman asked.

Kate recognized Mr. Kastan. He owned the jewelry shop on Market Street. It was just four doors away from Mr. Hillman's store.

"You can give me some aspirin," said Mr. Kastan. "But that won't cure my headache."

Mr. Hillman took a bottle out of a drawer. "What sort of headache do you have?" he asked politely.

"Shoplifters!" Mr. Kastan said. He banged his fist on the counter. "My store was hit by shoplifters again yesterday."

Kate gulped. So that's what she felt in the leather pouch. Mr. Kastan's jewelry!

"I'm sorry to hear that," Mr. Hillman said. "I got hit myself earlier this week."

"I don't know how they do it," Mr. Kastan said, shaking his head. "I was waiting on a customer, showing her some diamond rings. I had to go into my workshop for a minute. That was the only time I left the room. Then today I found out what was missing — a gold necklace and a silver ring."

60

"Do you think the lady took it?" Kate asked.

Mr. Kastan looked at her and smiled. "No, the mayor's wife is one of my best customers." Then he became angry again. "No, I think it's a gang of kids."

Kate bent down to pet Penny. She felt terrible. "I'm part of that gang," she thought. "I could be in trouble."

Kate got up and started walking to the door. "I'll see you later, Mr. Hillman," she said. She went out the door onto Market Street. She didn't want to meet Mike or Pete or Tracy. She decided to go to Dr. Marx's house. She couldn't get into trouble there.

Kate took the long way to his office. She didn't want to cut through the park. Mike, Pete, and Tracy would be looking for her there.

Kate was glad when she got to the office.

"Hi, Kate," Dr. Marx said. "I haven't seen you for a while."

"I've been sort of busy," Kate answered.

"So have I," said Dr. Marx. "I've seen four cats, three dogs, a sick guinea pig, and even a snake this afternoon. People choose so many kinds of animals for pets. The trouble is they can't always take care of them."

Kate heard the bell ring on his door. "I wonder what's next," she said.

A woman appeared with a large tom cat in

her arms. Kate saw right away that its ear was bleeding.

"I think you've been in a fight," Dr. Marx said to the cat.

"And I think my cat lost," said the woman.

Dr. Marx put the cat on the table, and the woman sat in the waiting room.

"Kate, you can help me," Dr. Marx said as he worked. "I have to put medicine on the wound and patch him up."

Dr. Marx handed Kate a glass medicine dropper. But Kate hadn't heard what he said. She was thinking about Major and the bag of stolen jewelry around his neck.

"Oh, no!" Kate jumped as the glass shattered on the floor. The dropper had fallen right out of her hand.

"It's all right, Kate," Dr. Marx said. "You clean it up, and I'll take care of the cat."

Kate felt miserable. She found a broom and swept up the glass. Then she went over the floor with a damp cloth. She sat quietly on the stool while Dr. Marx finished with the cat.

"All right, Kate, what's bothering you?" Dr. Marx asked when the woman was gone.

Kate said nothing.

"I know something's wrong," Dr. Marx insisted.

Kate looked up at him. I can't keep it to myself anymore, she decided. She began pouring out the whole story.

Dr. Marx sat down and listened carefully. Kate told him about Mike and Pete and Tracy. And about Mike poisoning Penny. Then she described the race and Major's pouch. Finally, she told him about Mr. Kastan's jewelry.

"Whew!" Dr. Marx said when she finished. "That was quite a story."

"It's not a story," Kate said. "It's the truth.

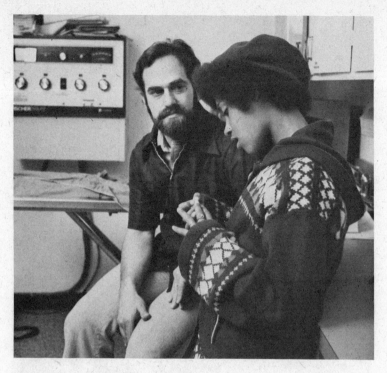

What am I going to do?"

Dr. Marx stood and paced the room. He was thinking hard. "I think you should go to the police, Kate," he said.

Kate sighed. She had thought about that a lot. But could they catch the shoplifters?

"I know you must be right, Dr. Marx," Kate said. She got up to leave. "But I can't prove they are the shoplifters. They have to get caught in the act. They have to be caught stealing."

Kate walked to the door. She turned around suddenly and faced Dr. Marx.

"And I'm going to set the trap!" she said.

The time was 3 p.m. exactly. Kate was already in the park. She had rushed there right after school.

"Today is the day," Kate told herself as she sat on a bench. She was determined to turn Mike, Tracy, and Pete over to the police. They had tried to poison Penny. And they were stealing from Mr. Hillman and Mr. Kastan. Kate hated to think of anything else they could be doing.

She looked down the sidewalk in both directions. There was no sign of Tracy, Mike, or Pete. Kate knew she had to go to the police today. But, first, she wanted to set the trap. I'm an insider now, she told herself. I can do more than anyone else to catch them.

Kate stood up and paced the sidewalk. She was really nervous! What if they suspected her? She had run off too quickly yesterday. What if they had already trained Major to run to Pete? Then they wouldn't need her anymore.

"Hey, Kate, it's good to see you again!" Kate whirled around. It was Mike's voice calling from behind.

"Tracy and I missed you yesterday

afternoon," Mike said. Kate could see he was angry with her. "You were supposed to meet us in the park, remember?"

Kate nodded her head in agreement. Then she bent down and petted Major. "But I did my part in the race," she insisted. "I whistled for Major exactly the way you told me."

"You were supposed to come to the park with me and Major afterward," Pete said.

"That's right, Kate," added Tracy. "You left Pete in a real mess. He couldn't get Major to go to the park with him."

Kate laughed about that to herself. "I didn't know I would cause trouble," she said. "I just remembered that I was late getting home. I could have gotten in trouble with my family."

Mike didn't seem happy with Kate's answer. "It wasn't only a game we were playing, Kate. It's important that we can trust you."

Kate swallowed hard. Don't tell me any more, she said to herself. I can't go on acting stupid if you do.

"I am sorry, Mike," Kate said. "Give me another chance, please. Major and I will do our part right this time. I promise."

Mike looked at Tracy and Pete. "Well, how about it?" he asked. Kate was really nervous now. If they said yes, she could use her plan. But if they said no, she wouldn't know what to

do. To hide her nervousness, Kate looked down and petted Major. He was such a great dog.

"You know, she's the only one the dog likes," Tracy said.

"I think we're better off with her. What could we do without her?" asked Pete.

Good, Kate thought. But what would Mike say? She held her breath. He still seemed unsure. "I don't know if I trust her," he said. "Kate, do you promise to do just what I say?"

"Major and I will do our parts," Kate answered. She hated to lie, even to Mike. But her answer wasn't really a lie. It just didn't mean the same thing to Mike that it did to her.

"Then, we'll do things differently this afternoon," Mike began. "Kate will be on her own with Major. Pete will come with me."

Kate's heart pounded in her throat. This afternoon! They were shoplifting today! She'd have to work fast.

Mike continued. "We'll use the same places as yesterday. Mike looked at his watch. "It's four o'clock now. Kate, you'll be on Elm Street one block from the park. Be there at 4:30 sharp."

Kate's mind raced. I can't run to the police station and back to Elm Street that fast, she thought.

"I can't be there at 4:30, Mike," she said. Kate tried to sound sad. "Please, can't you make it five o'clock? I really want to play the relay race today."

"Why can't you be there?" Mike asked. He sounded angry again.

"I have to run an errand for my friend, Dr. Marx. I promised him that I would do it."

Tracy tried to calm Mike down. "What's wrong with five o'clock, Mike? Give Kate a chance. We need her."

"All right," Mike said. "But you'd better be there at five sharp!"

Kate glanced down at her watch. "Then I should be going right now."

Kate started out of the park. She knew she didn't have a minute to spare. She had to get to the police station fast.

Kate ran to the opposite side of the park. The police station was there. She was getting more scared. What if the police didn't believe her? What if she got in trouble for helping the kids yesterday?

At twenty minutes past four, Kate reached

the steps of the police station. She ran inside. A policeman was sitting at a desk in the middle of the huge room.

"What can I do for you today?" he asked Kate.

"I need to talk to the police," Kate gasped. She was almost out of breath from running. "It's about shoplifters. I have some inside information."

The policeman stared at Kate for a minute. Then he picked up the telephone and spoke to someone.

"Officer Morgan will be out in a minute," he said to Kate. "He wants to talk to you."

Kate sat down on a hard bench. Her heart was pounding. Soon, a tall policeman came into the room.

"I'm Officer Morgan. I hear you know something about the shoplifters. Follow me."

"Yes, sir," Kate said as she followed him into another room. Officer Morgan sat down behind his desk, and Kate took the chair in front of it.

"OK, shoot," said Officer Morgan. Kate's eyes opened wide. She didn't know what to say.

Officer Morgan started to laugh. "I mean, let's hear your story — from the beginning."

In a shaky voice, Kate began to tell Officer Morgan how it all started.

Soon they were plotting a trap together.

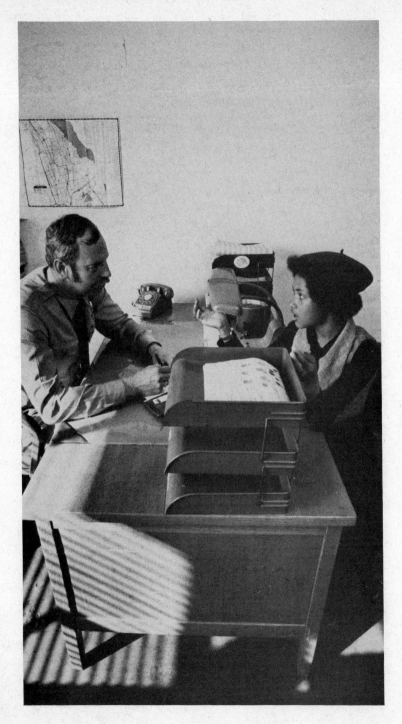

CHAPTER

Officer Morgan dropped Kate off three blocks from Elm Street. There wasn't much time left. She had to get to her station in five minutes. As she ran toward it, Kate went over their plan in her mind. She was supposed to follow Mike's instructions. She would wait on Elm Street to whistle for Major. But she would whistle as soon as Mike and Pete appeared. She wouldn't give them time to stash the stolen things in the leather pouch. Major would run straight to Kate, and Mike and Pete would be caught red-handed. Then Kate would go to the park with Major. She would wait there for Officer Morgan to meet her.

"It's got to work," Kate whispered. She arrived at the corner of Elm Street and glanced at her watch. It was exactly five o'clock. Kate looked up Elm Street. There, five blocks away, she saw Tracy and Major. Kate let out a sigh of relief. So far, the plan was working perfectly. Now all I have to do is wait, Kate thought. She glanced up the street again at Tracy. Tracy waved her hand and Kate waved back.

"I wonder what Pete and Mike are up to now," Kate said quietly to herself. "Maybe they're stealing from Mr. Hillman and Mr. Kastan again." That made her blood boil. Pete must be shoplifting, too. They wanted to make a double haul today. Well, Kate thought, it will be the right day for them to get caught!

Suddenly, Kate saw that ten minutes had passed. She'd better be on the alert. When Mike and Pete came, she'd have to give the whistle. If she was too late, Major would be carrying the stolen goods. And Kate would be the one caught red-handed!

She fixed her eyes on Tracy and Major. Pete and Mike could show up any time now. Just then, Mike came rushing around the corner. But Pete wasn't with him.

"Oh, no!" Kate said. "What should I do now? Should I wait for Pete? Or should I whistle for Major?" If she waited too long, Mike would stash the stolen goods in Major's pouch.

Kate wet her lips and got ready to whistle. Mike was bending down over Major. Then, Kate saw Pete dashing across the street to join Tracy and Mike.

Kate whistled. It was the loudest whistle she'd ever made in her life! Major jumped to his feet and started to run. But Mike grabbed him. He grabbed one of Major's back legs and held on!

Kate whistled again, as hard as she could.

Major was struggling to get away. Kate saw Mike's face getting red and angry.

Suddenly, Major turned on Mike. Kate saw Mike jump away from the dog, holding his hand. Major had bit him! He wanted to escape.

Then everything happened at once. Major ran swiftly down the street to Kate. Kate saw Officer Morgan's car pull onto Elm Street. It screeched to a stop near Tracy, Mike, and Pete.

The three took off running, and Officer Morgan leaped from his car in hot pursuit. Kate lost sight of them as they all dashed around a corner.

Then Kate looked back at Major. He was racing full speed to her. Something flashed in Kate's mind. It was like a bad dream coming back. This was just like the time Bonnie was killed. She had whistled and Bonnie came running. And then the car....

Kate jerked her head and looked at the street. There *was* a car speeding up the side street. Major was only a block away! Kate knew what to do without even thinking.

"Major!" she screamed as loud as she could. "Halt, Major! Halt!"

Kate saw Major hesitate. The car flashed across the street.

Kate's heart was beating fast. Did Major stop in time? The car shot past her and across Elm Street. Kate saw Major sitting on the opposite corner. He was waiting obediently for her to call him again.

Tears of relief came to Kate's eyes. She looked down the street both ways. Then she called out softly, "Here, Major."

The collie came running up to her. Kate knelt down and hugged him over and over. "You're all right, aren't you, Major?" she asked. Major gave a soft whine and rubbed his head in her hand. Kate laughed and cried at the same time. Major was fine! Kate forgot all about Tracy and Mike and Pete and Officer Morgan. All she could do was hold Major and think about Bonnie. Kate had thought fast enough this time. She had saved Major's life!

"Come on, Major," Kate called. "You and I are going to the park."

Kate walked slowly to the park entrance with Major. What had happened to Officer Morgan? She wished she knew. If only she could help

him in some way. Then a horrible thought came into her mind. What if Mike and Pete and Tracy had escaped? What if they had gotten away and were waiting for her in the park right now?

All of a sudden, Kate was afraid. She didn't want to take the chance. If Mike and Pete and Tracy had gotten away, they might be in the park. But if Officer Morgan had caught them, he couldn't be there yet.

"We'd better take a long way there, Major," Kate said. She turned off Elm Street and onto a side road. Major followed her closely.

Kate and Major walked around and around in a circle. After ten minutes, Kate decided it was time to go to the park.

"I wonder who will be waiting." Kate said. Now she and Major were walking down the main path of the park. "I'm so glad you're with me, Major," she said. Just then, Kate heard something that made her jump. Someone was calling her name!

"Kate, Kate, over here!" the voice called.

With a sick feeling in her stomach, Kate turned around to see who was calling. It was Officer Morgan! He stepped onto the path and held out his hand to her.

"Congratulations, Kate," he said and smiled. "You and I have just caught three shoplifters."

"What happened?" Kate eagerly asked Officer Morgan. Now she felt safe and happy again.

"They were pretty fast runners for me," Officer Morgan answered. "I thought for a while they might get away. But it was their own greed that caught them."

"What do you mean?" Kate asked.

"Well, the one named Pete dropped the bag he was carrying. There were some stolen things stashed in it. Then the boy named Mike tried to stop and pick up the bag. That's when I caught up with them. Once I had Mike, the others were easy to catch."

"Where are they now?" Kate glanced around uneasily.

"They're safe and sound in the police station," said the officer. "And now, I'm going to get you home safe and sound. Let's go."

Kate and Officer Morgan started walking out of the park. Major followed along behind them.

"What will happen to those kids?" Kate asked.

"That all depends on what the judge says," Officer Morgan answered. "And on what else they may have done. I have a feeling that Tracy and Pete might talk. But not that Mike. He's a bad character."

"Mike is the one who poisoned Penny, Mr. Hillman's German shepherd," Kate said. Then she thought of Major.

"But what about Major? What will happen to him?" Kate asked.

Officer Morgan bent down and petted the dog. "Major can go back to his real owner now."

"What?" Kate said, surprised.

"Yes, Major was stolen, too," said the officer. "I guess that's why he didn't get along very well with those kids. An officer at the station checked through the missing animal file. We found a dog that fits Major's description exactly."

Kate stopped walking and bent down to pet him. "I'll miss you, Major. But I guess you'll be happy to go home to your owner. You've had enough excitement for a while."

Officer Morgan laughed. "I think the same goes for you, Kate." They had just reached the police car. "Get in and I'll take you home now."

Kate starting getting into the car. But just then, she saw Julie strolling down the street. Julie was carrying a small Scottie dog in her arms.

"Hi, Julie," Kate called out.

"Hi, Kate," Julie said. She gave Officer Morgan a funny look.

"It's okay, Julie," Kate laughed. "He's not arresting me."

Julie smiled, relieved. "I brought Tartan to the park for you to see."

"Can you bring him back tomorrow? Please, Julie?" Kate asked. "I have to go straight home now."

Julie still looked puzzled. Kate got into the car. Then she called out to Julie. "I'll tell you all about it tomorrow."

"OK, tomorrow after school," Julie agreed. She waved good-bye as the police car drove away.

"Is she a friend of yours?" Officer Morgan asked as they drove down the street.

"I hope so," Kate answered. Then she changed her mind. "Yes, she is my friend."

In a short time, the police car arrived in front of Kate's house. When Officer Morgan got out of the car, Major let out a soft moan.

"Don't worry, Major," said Kate. "I won't forget to say good-bye. Kate leaned across the seat and rubbed the collie's head. "I wish...," Kate started to say. Then she stopped. It was no use. Major was somebody else's dog.

Kate petted Major one last time. Then she got out of the car. She walked up to her house with Officer Morgan.

"Kate! Is everything all right? What happened?" asked her father when he opened the door.

Kate introduced her father to Officer Morgan. Then the three of them went into the house.

"Kate, where have you been?" asked her mother. She stopped short when she noticed the policeman.

Officer Morgan said, "I think I'd better tell you everything. I don't want you to get the wrong idea about Kate."

Kate laughed. Her parents really looked so worried. Did they imagine she'd done something wrong?

"Kate visited the police station this afternoon," Officer Morgan began. "And she had quite a story to tell."

Kate relaxed in a chair and listened to the officer talking. He told her parents all about Tracy, Mike, and Pete, and their arrest. Kate got excited all over again hearing the story. It sounded even more dangerous than when it happened.

"Well, Kate," her father said when the officer finished. "We're very proud of you. It took a lot of courage to turn in those shoplifters. Some kids would probably have been afraid to say anything."

Kate squirmed in her chair. She didn't feel like a hero. She had done it because she was angry at Mike and Pete and Tracy. They had gotten what they deserved.

Officer Morgan stood up to leave. "I'll call you when I hear more about their case, Kate. And thanks again for your assistance."

He went out the door, and Kate and her parents sat down again.

94

"There's something else that happened,"
Kate told them. "Something that Officer
Morgan couldn't tell you."

"What is it?" asked her father.

"Well," said Kate. "Part of our plan was that
Major had to run to me. But when he did, I
remembered what happened to Bonnie. So I
looked carefully down the street. When I saw a
car coming, I yelled 'Halt' to Major. He obeyed
me and waited on the corner. I saved his life."

"That's wonderful," said her father. "You did just the right thing."

"Yes, you did," agreed her mother.

Kate smiled at them. "I feel I can trust myself," she said. "I know how to take care of a dog now."

Kate's father leaned over and put his arm around her. "Well, then, he said. "I think it's time you got another dog."

"I do, too," added her mother.

Kate looked at them and said, "Yes, it's really time!"